D1616396

THE PARABLE OF THE GOLDEN PATHWAY

WRITTEN BY

JENNY PHILLIPS

ILLUSTRATED BY

DAN BURR

Music CD:
"Come to the Pathway" by Jenny Phillips. Arranged by Daniel Lee. Vocal by Jenny Phillips.
© 2010 Mohrgüd Music (BMI)
"The Kingdom of Light" by Jenny Phillips and Tyler Castleton. Arranged by Daniel Lee. Vocal by Matt Bardsley.
© 2010 Mohrgüd Music (BMI)/Diamond Aire Music (ASCAP)
"Return to Him" by Jenny Phillips. Arranged by Daniel Lee. Vocal by Julie Yardley.
© 2010 Mohrgüd Music (BMI)
"Firm in the Faith" by Jenny Phillips and Tyler Castleton. Arranged by Tyler Castleton. Vocal by Hayley Anderson.
© 2008 Jenny Phillips Music/Diamond Aire Music (ASCAP)
"Keepers of His Light" by Jenny Phillips and Tyler Castleton. Arranged by Tyler Castleton.
© 2007 Shadow Mountain/Diamond Aire Music (ASCAP)

Visit us at DeseretBook.com

Phillips, Jenny (Jenny Harris)

The parable of the golden pathway / by Jenny Phillips ; illustrated by Dan Burr.
p. cm.
Summary: When the Light Maker's messenger comes to Sarah's town and invites everyone to come and live in the Kingdom of Light, many accept the offer and embark on the golden pathway. Throughout her journey, Sarah learns that, though the pathway may not always be easy, the blessings are priceless and eternal.
ISBN 978-1-60641-651-8 (hardbound : alk. paper)
1. Christian pilgrims and pilgrimages—Fiction. 2. Christian life—Fiction. 3. Christian fiction, American. 4. Allegories. I. Title.
PS3616.H458P37 2010
813'.6—dc22 2009052500

Printed in China
Four Colour Print Group
10 9 8 7 6 5 4 3 2 1

CONTENTS

CHAPTER 1

THE LIGHT MAKER'S MESSENGER

Sarah had grown up hearing the legend of the Light Maker. The stories said he was the maker of light, who ruled a kingdom that was the most beautiful and mighty of all. It was a legend that had always enthralled Sarah. One day Sarah's sister, Tabitha, and her brother, Ori, came running into the cottage out of breath, shouting that a messenger sent by the Light Maker had just arrived in town.

Sarah shot up from the kitchen table at once. "What?" she cried. "A messenger from the Light Maker? In our town?"

"Come on," cried Ori, grabbing his sister's hand. "Everyone is gathered in the town square."

Sarah, Ori, and Tabitha hurried to the square and found the messenger preparing to speak.

When he spoke, it seemed to Sarah that her heart filled with light, and peace flowed through her. Somehow she knew this man was truly a messenger from the Light Maker. She knew then as well that the Light Maker must really exist.

"The Light Maker," the messenger said, "has sent me to invite you all to his glorious kingdom to live."

Sarah heard the boy next to her snicker. "Crazy man," he muttered under his breath. "There is no Light Maker."

Many people just shook their heads and left the town square.

"Will anyone accept this journey? Will anyone come to the Kingdom of Light?" the messenger asked.

Sarah did not hesitate. "I will!" she declared, stepping forward quickly.

“And I,” said Ori, stepping up next to his sister and putting his arm around her. He looked back at their sister, Tabitha. She smiled and stepped forward with them. “Count me in too.”

Although many people chose not to make the journey, many others joined Sarah, Ori, and Tabitha.

Later that day, at the edge of the forest, the messenger met everyone who had chosen to make the journey. He showed them a golden pathway they had never seen before.

“This is the Light Maker’s pathway. It leads directly to the Kingdom of Light,” the messenger explained. “Unfortunately, the Light Maker has many enemies, powerful warriors of darkness, who try to prevent anyone from reaching the Kingdom of Light. The Light Maker has asked that I give these gifts to you to help you on your journey. If you follow the instructions that go with them, you are assured a successful journey to the Kingdom of Light.”

The messenger presented Sarah, Ori, Tabitha, and each of the other travelers at the edge of the forest with a beautifully crafted sword and shield.

"The Light Maker's instructions are to keep the shield with you at all times. Do not carry it in your bags, but keep it where you can use it at an instant's notice. The shield will protect you well from the enemy, but it cannot be taken off the golden pathway," the messenger explained.

He then pointed to their swords. "These swords are filled with the Light Maker's light and power, which are much stronger than all of the combined powers of his enemies."

Sarah held up her sword and marveled. The blade was incredible. It was made of the purest crystal she had ever seen and was filled with a brilliant light.

The messenger continued his instructions. "To keep the light and power strong in your sword, you must practice with it every day. The power in your sword will fade unless you use it regularly. And walking off the path—even a step—will immediately weaken the power in your sword. You will not be able to complete the journey if your sword does not remain strong."

"Only the golden pathway will lead you to the Kingdom of Light," the messenger said boldly. "Any other path will lead you away from the Kingdom of Light. Stay on the golden pathway, even when it's difficult to understand why."

The messenger looked at the small group, and his eyes filled with tears. "You are more valuable to the Light Maker than you know. He awaits your arrival," he said. "He will help you complete your journey. Call to him whenever you need help, and you will always receive it. "

With their swords and shields in their hands, Sarah, Ori, Tabitha, and the rest began their journey along the golden pathway.

CHAPTER 2

THE LAND OF COTTAGES

The golden pathway soon opened up into a great valley that extended farther than the eye could see. Rolling brown hills were dotted with little stone cottages, and many different pathways wound through brightly decorated open-air markets and ornamented buildings.

As Sarah, Ori, and Tabitha continued on the golden pathway through the Land of Cottages, they made friends with others traveling on the Light Maker's path. While the Light Maker's path was narrow, in the Land of Cottages it meandered throughout the valley, giving the travelers a wide variety of places to visit. They enjoyed their journey very much, but many of the people who lived in the Land of Cottages made fun of them.

"Why are you carrying those silly swords and shields? Stay here with us. There are so many other pathways to try in this land," they cried. "Look at this glittering pathway. There's always something on this path that will entertain you. Come and try it."

"I cannot leave the golden pathway," Ori would reply with a smile. "I am going to the Kingdom of Light."

And the three siblings happily moved forward along the golden pathway.

But one day, Tabitha noticed something about the people traveling on the golden pathway through the Land of Cottages. Some were hiding their shields in their bags at times. And some people were leaving the path and their shields altogether and returning later. Tabitha asked a girl on the pathway about it.

"I'll tell you a secret," said the girl. "Boys are much more attracted to you when you don't carry your shield with you all the time."

"But the messenger told us not to put the shield in our bags—and doesn't going off the path make your sword grow dimmer?" Tabitha asked.

The girl shrugged. "The only difference I've noticed is that I get a lot more attention from the boys."

Tabitha had not been able to catch the attention of a particular boy traveling on the golden pathway. Oh, how she wanted that boy to notice her! So she decided to hide her shield in her bag instead of carrying it the next day as she walked beside him.

She saw him notice her, and secretly, she smiled. The very next day, he asked her to go to a banquet with him. When he told her that the banquet was on another pathway (a cute little one lined with brown cobblestones), she hesitated.

"Don't worry," the boy said. "The Light Maker's golden pathway will be here when you return, just the same as when you left it." The boy grinned knowingly at Tabitha. "There are more exciting things off the pathway than on it!"

Tabitha wondered what those things might be.

"Come on. The banquet isn't really that far from here."

So Tabitha decided to go with him and return to the golden pathway as soon as the banquet was over. But the instant Tabitha stepped off the pathway, the shield pulled her bag to the ground, and it became so heavy she couldn't lift it. When she remembered that the shields couldn't be taken off the golden pathway, she hesitated. But the boy was walking away from her.

"There's no sign of dark warriors," Tabitha thought. "I'll just leave the shield here. I won't be gone long, and I'll get it as soon as I come back."

The banquet was exciting, and Tabitha noticed more boys paying attention to her than ever before, even after she returned to the golden pathway.

When Sarah saw the attention Tabitha was getting, she was tempted to hide her shield, too. Sarah had become very fond of a boy named David who was traveling with their group. They were friends, but Sarah wondered if she would be more attractive to him if she hid her shield. But she decided to trust the Light Maker's instructions.

Ori and Sarah practiced with their swords every day. Though it meant finding time among her many daily tasks, Sarah enjoyed the practice. Every time she picked up her sword, she felt the strength of the Light Maker flow through her. The thought of reaching his kingdom and seeing him face-to-face thrilled her. Sarah tried to get Tabitha to practice too, but Tabitha always seemed to have more pressing chores to do, and most days she chose not to practice at all.

CHAPTER 3

THE JEWELED PATH INTO THE FOREST

Soon the golden pathway led the travelers out of the Land of Cottages and around the outskirts of a large, beautiful forest. One day, a beautiful girl named Sapphira walked with Ori as they traveled.

"Have you ever taken one of the pathways into the forest?" Sapphira asked Ori as she put a wildflower in her long, flowing blonde hair. "The forest is absolutely amazing. You've got to see it at least once."

Ori saw a pathway ahead that led into the trees. Jewels of all colors paved the pathway and sparkled in the sun.

"I'd better not," Ori answered her. "Besides, look way up there on that mountain," he said, squinting and pointing far into the distance. "The Light Maker's path actually goes through the fair forest at the top of that mountain. I'll see inside the forest when I get there."

"It will take weeks to get there. Why not see it now?" Sapphira asked.

"Because I'm following the Light Maker's instructions," Ori said simply.

Sapphira laughed. "Ori, it doesn't hurt to have a little fun sometimes."

"That's good, because I have fun all the time," Ori replied with a big grin.

"Really?" Sapphira asked with raised eyebrows.

Ori stopped and turned to Sapphira. "Really," he replied. "I want to go to the Kingdom of Light, Sapphira. I'm so happy on this path. The people I see go off the path don't seem happy afterward."

Sapphira shook her head. "Suit yourself." She laughed as she dropped her shield and skipped away down the jeweled path.

But the next day Sapphira returned to the golden pathway and walked with Ori. He listened to her as she talked about the jeweled path and what could be seen in the forest. And the day after that, as they talked and walked together, he started to wonder—just a little bit—about that path into the forest.

Ori knew he shouldn't spend time with a girl who was so careless about her shield. But she was beautiful, and he enjoyed talking to her. He started thinking about following her into the forest. At first it was only an occasional thought, but he thought about it enough that one day Sapphira's big, beautiful eyes made him forget the journey he was on. He left his shield behind and followed her just a few steps onto the jewel-studded pathway. It didn't seem like much. Walking along the jeweled pathway with Sapphira was incredibly exciting. But when he returned to the golden path, he felt terrible. Try as he might, he couldn't shake the bad feelings he had.

At first Ori didn't venture far enough into the forest to lose sight of the golden pathway. Soon, however, the golden pathway seemed to grow dull and less appealing than it had been previously. He walked farther and farther into the forest before returning to the Light Maker's path. His thoughts turned more often to the jeweled pathway than to the Kingdom of Light. When Sarah wanted him to help her practice with her sword, he made excuses. Most days he preferred to think about the jeweled pathway instead. He just didn't feel the urgency of practicing. Where were the dark warriors? Why should he miss out on so much by always staying on the golden path?

One day Ori went with Sapphira into the forest farther than he ever had before. Suddenly, he heard a bugle echoing through the trees. The call to battle! Panicked, he raced toward the golden pathway. He could see it in the distance. And he could see the dark warriors attacking. Sarah was outnumbered, but she was wielding her sword heroically.

Ori was almost to the path when he was cut off and surrounded by dark warriors. He lifted his sword, but it had grown dim and its power weak. The sword of a dark warrior quickly shattered it. Ori wished he had his shield, for he had nothing to prevent the dark warrior's sword from slicing into his side. Ori fell to the ground in terrible pain, and the dark warriors bound him in heavy chains and carried him off. The dark warriors bound Sapphira, too. Ori looked at the pieces of his broken sword lying in the dirt. The dull crystal held no light.

On the golden pathway, the travelers prevailed against the dark warriors, who fled from their shining swords. Word quickly spread that Ori had followed Sapphira into the forest and that he hadn't been seen after the battle. Tabitha's and Sarah's hearts were broken. They hoped Ori and Sapphira would emerge from the forest and catch up to them. They didn't know they had been carried off by the dark warriors to their awful prison.

CHAPTER 4

THE DARK MIST

By the time Sarah's journey had taken her past the forest, many of her friends were no longer with her. But she was enjoying the company of those who remained—especially David. He was always whistling, singing, or laughing. But what Sarah loved most was talking with him about the Light Maker. When she listened to him, she could feel the desire to reach the Kingdom of Light burn strong within her. David made her *want* to stay on the path. And as she grew to know him, she saw that he wasn't the kind of boy who would be interested in a girl who hid her shield or left it to go off the path. She was glad she had decided not to do those things. She knew she would have been ashamed if David had seen her hide her shield.

Sarah and David were friends, but Sarah wondered if he was as fond of her as she was of him. Once Sarah thought she had caught David watching her with a smile on his face when she was practicing with her sword, but she wasn't sure.

One morning Sarah and Tabitha were walking together, laughing and talking. They turned a corner, and the two sisters were immediately overtaken by a thick, dark mist.

"Sarah, I can't see you," shouted Tabitha, struggling to be heard over the roar of rushing water nearby.

Sarah couldn't see anything either, so she quickly unsheathed her sword, and its light lit up the sky.

"Tabitha, hold up your sword," Sarah instructed.

Obeying her sister, Tabitha took her sword out of its sheath and held it up. Struck with fear and sadness, she realized her sword was too dim to overcome the darkness. Tabitha could not even see Sarah.

"I can't see anything with my sword!" Tabitha cried.

Sarah put her arm around her sister. "Here, I'll hold my sword up for you so you can see."

Tabitha squinted into the dark but saw nothing. "I still can't see anything, Sarah. I think . . . I think maybe only you can see through this mist by your own light. I will just have to hold on to you as we travel through this mist."

"Tabitha," Sarah said slowly, her heart racing in fear at what the light of her sword revealed, "there's a river filled with whirlpools and raging currents in front of us. It goes farther than I can see. The only way across is a path of golden stones. Because there is only room for one person on each stone, we can't jump at the same time. You won't be able to hold on to me."

Tabitha turned and walked back out of the mist. Her sister followed her.

"I'm going back to the Land of Cottages," Tabitha declared.

"No!" cried Sarah. "You can't go back!"

"Why not? I liked it there. Besides, I can't go forward even if I wanted to. My sword isn't strong enough."

"The Light Maker will help you!" Sarah pleaded.

Tabitha sighed. "No, he won't."

"But don't you remember? The messenger said the Light Maker would do everything he could to help us. I know he will help you if you call to him!"

Tabitha wondered if her sister was right. She seemed to remember what the messenger had said. It had been a long time ago. But the journey to the Kingdom of Light didn't seem that important anymore. She had never seen this Light Maker. Why did he want her to keep her shield with her always? Why couldn't she travel any pathway she wanted to? She took a deep breath and made up her mind.

"Don't worry about me," Tabitha stated. "I'll be fine." And with that, she put down her shield and disappeared along another path.

Sarah was alone. A tear slid down her cheek as she looked at Tabitha's abandoned shield. But then with determination, Sarah stepped back into the dark mist and turned toward the dark river. She held up her sword to light her way, and she jumped to the first golden stone.

Dark, billowing clouds swirled around her as she traveled across the river, jumping from stone to stone. The wind became so strong that it whipped her long black hair into her face and knocked her off balance. She fell heavily onto a stone and then into the icy water. Her leg throbbed as she pulled herself, shivering, back onto the stone.

As she jumped to the next stone, she heard voices in the wind.

"Why are you here all alone in the cold and the wind?"

"Why do you carry that burdensome shield? It's kept you from enjoying so much!"

"This pathway isn't the right way!"

"There is no Light Maker!"

"There is no reason to stay on this path—you're a fool!"

"Your sister's having a great time while you're here struggling. It's not worth it!"

For a moment, Sarah felt the awful power of despair. But then she gripped her sword and held it higher. She instantly felt a strong power and a deep peace flow through her, and she saw the sword's magnificent light cut through the darkness. She heard the messenger's words in her heart once again: "The Light Maker awaits your arrival."

"I am coming," Sarah cried into the wind.

Sarah jumped to the next rock, her legs trembling. She felt terribly weak. But relying on the strength in her sword, she managed to keep jumping from stone to stone.

It seemed to take hours, but finally Sarah's feet touched dry land again. She had reached the other side of the river!

CHAPTER 5

THE SMOOTH, SILVER PATHWAY

Shaking with exhaustion, Sarah looked ahead of her and saw that the golden pathway wound up a high mountain. She was so tired she could hardly lift her feet. She sat down in the middle of the path and began to cry. Why was the Light Maker asking so much of her? Why would he make the path this hard?

"Don't worry," a voice called to her. "There is another way."

Sarah looked up and saw a boy about her age standing a short distance away on a path that was paved with smooth silver. Beside the boy were two girls who smiled at Sarah.

"This path," the boy said, pointing to the silver path he was on, "is headed in the same direction you are going. Do you want to travel with us?"

Sarah was confused. "But the Light Maker's messenger said the golden pathway was the only pathway that led to the Kingdom of Light and that all others led away from it."

"Sure, there are some paths you should avoid," said the girl with red hair. "But this one is easier than the golden pathway. You can always get on the golden pathway again later, once you've gone around the mountain."

The girls and the boy looked nice and seemed happy. Sarah felt alone without Ori and Tabitha. The thought of having friends on her journey was appealing. She walked closer to the silver pathway.

"Part of the problem is your shield," said the redheaded girl. "When you carry it around with you everywhere, it stresses you out. You become uptight. And it's hard to feel beautiful lugging that shield around with you. No wonder you're unhappy and crying. Just lay your shield down for a while. You'll feel better."

"I . . . I'm not sure," Sarah replied. She looked at the two girls, and she felt confused. They had no shields with them, and yet they seemed happy. They were beautiful. And Sarah didn't feel happy or beautiful at the moment. She felt alone. She wanted to feel happy and beautiful. Maybe carrying her shield around *did* make her uptight. Maybe it wouldn't hurt to lay it down for a while.

Sarah walked to the point where the silver pathway diverged from the golden one. A soft wind blew through the trees, and brightly colored flowers grew along the sides of the silver path. She suddenly longed for the acceptance and easiness these companions and this pathway seemed to offer.

Sarah put a foot on the silver pathway. Immediately, her shield felt much heavier. Her sword also felt suddenly weaker. The change in her sword was so very small, though, that it was easy to dismiss. In fact, come to think of it, she wasn't sure she had really felt her sword change at all. Sarah thought about how her sister, Tabitha, had gradually lost her desire for the Kingdom of Light. She realized that once she put both feet on this path, she would become more confused and lose her desire for the Kingdom of Light, just as Tabitha had.

"I have to trust the messenger," Sarah said to herself. "I have to trust his instruction never to step off the path."

Making her decision, she put her foot back on the golden pathway.

"I don't understand completely why the Light Maker told me to never step off the pathway, but he did," she said to the two girls and the boy. "And I trust him." She looked at all three steadily. "You should trust him too," she said gently.

The redheaded girl and the boy laughed and walked away down the silver path. The other girl, however, looked at her for a long moment before she turned and walked slowly after her friends.

Alone again, Sarah walked along the golden pathway to where it began to climb steeply up the mountain. She knew she didn't have the strength to climb. Her leg had been cut and bruised when she'd fallen on the stone in the river, and it ached with every step.

Suddenly, Sarah heard a noise. Behind her she saw dark warriors streaming across the river towards her. They were shooting blazing arrows into the sky. One landed right next to Sarah. She quickly held up her shield for protection. The fiery arrows rained down all around her. There were so many—hundreds, it seemed. They beat angrily against her shield as she crouched beneath it.

Sarah squeezed her eyes shut and called out to the Light Maker.

"Help me! Please help me!" Her voice felt weak.

Just then, a warm wind wrapped gently around her and filled her with peace. The arrows stopped beating against her shield.

Soon all was quiet. When she dared look out from under her shield, the dark warriors were retreating across the river. She was safe. The Light Maker had helped her, just as he said he would. All night as she slept at the base of the mountain, she felt wrapped in peace and warmth. In the morning, a voice woke her. It was David.

"Sarah," he cried, running towards her. He had just crossed the river. They talked about how difficult the journey had been across the terrible river and rejoiced that they had both reached the other side safely. David then saw Sarah's leg, bruised and bleeding, and took in the rest of the scene. Charred arrows littered the path around where Sarah's shield had been. He bent down, reached into his bag for a bit of cloth, and tenderly bandaged Sarah's calf. His gentle eyes met hers.

"Sarah," David whispered, "you are very brave."

CHAPTER 6

TO THE KINGDOM OF LIGHT

As Sarah and David rested at the base of the mountain, many of their friends crossed the river and joined them. Sarah was especially thrilled to see one person in particular.

"Ori!" she shouted as her brother came running up from the river.

"Sarah!" he cried as he threw his arms around her. "I was carried off by the dark warriors to their terrible prison. I was miserable there. Finally I cried out to the Light Maker." Ori's voice broke. "Sarah, the Light Maker broke my chains and freed me. He restored my sword and filled it with light again. I have stayed on his path ever since. I haven't let anything distract me from going to the Kingdom of Light. If it weren't for the Light Maker's help . . ."

"I know," said Sarah. "I have felt him helping me many times on the journey too. What about Tabitha?" Sarah asked. "Have you seen her?"

Sorrow filled Ori's eyes. "Yes. But she wouldn't come back to the golden pathway. The light in her sword is almost gone. I know the Light Maker would help her if she would just call to him."

The hearts of the two siblings ached for Tabitha, and they longed for their sister to change her mind and join them.

In the meantime, a messenger from the Light Maker arrived to help guide the travelers over the mountain. They rested for a time until they were ready to start climbing the golden pathway that now led over the mountain. They all gathered together.

"I bet the view is beautiful at the top," said Ori, looking up at the mountain.

The Light Maker's messenger smiled. "You can see the Kingdom of Light from the top of the mountain. It is not far now."

A voice suddenly called out behind them. "Wait for us!"

It was the boy and the redheaded girl and her friend from the silver pathway. Out of breath, they quickly reached the group and spoke to Sarah.

"We thought about what you said," the redheaded girl explained. "We want to follow the Light Maker's instructions like you. Can we travel with your group?"

Sarah thought her heart would burst. "Of course!" she cried, hugging them.

Sarah glimpsed David watching her. This time she was sure he was watching her. And the way David was looking at her and smiling made Sarah suddenly feel completely beautiful.

"To the Kingdom of Light!" Ori cried as the group started up the mountain.

"To the Kingdom of Light!" Sarah and the others called back with a laugh as they began the last leg of their journey to meet the Light Maker.

EPILOGUE

Tabitha chose not to make the journey to the Kingdom of Light. Instead she journeyed along the pathways of the Land of Cottages, looking for others to entertain her and distract her from the emptiness and longing she often felt inside. Although she did find momentary pleasure and attention and excitement, nothing in that land ever made her feel truly beautiful or happy. And the flat, wide pathways she chose never challenged her to grow or become strong.

All journeys eventually bring us to a final destination—a destination that once reached can not be changed. Tabitha's final destination was a place prepared for those who did not honor their shields on their journey and chose not to return to the golden pathway. Tabitha's final destination was one where no one was united in marriage forever. Before she got to that final destination, Tabitha had to spend much time in the dark warriors' terrible prison. While there, she endured much anguish, especially when she came to see that dishonoring her shield had not only kept her from seeing the beauty and sweetness and truth of the golden pathway but had also made her an unwitting agent of the dark warriors.

Sarah and David took the last step of their journey on the golden pathway hand in hand. They stood in front of a beautiful golden gate. Sarah could see magnificent castle spires and beautiful mountains rising beyond the gates. They had reached their final destination. They had reached the Kingdom of Light!

The Light Maker opened the gate wide, and the couple ran into his open arms. Then he placed brilliant gold crowns upon their heads. Sarah felt completely beautiful. She was glorious, majestic—perfect in every way.

The Light Maker himself performed Sarah and David's marriage. On that day David told Sarah how grateful he was that she had kept the shield close to her on her journey. Then he read to her:

"Who can find a virtuous woman? for her price is far above rubies. The heart of her husband doth safely trust in her. . . . She girdeth her loins with strength. . . . She openeth her mouth with wisdom; and in her tongue is the law of kindness. . . . Her children arise up, and call her blessed; her husband also, and he praiseth her" (Proverbs 31:10–28).

REFLECTIONS FROM JENNY

Above all, taking the shield of faith, wherewith ye shall be able to quench all the fiery darts of the wicked. And take . . . the sword of the Spirit, which is the word of God.

Ephesians 6:16–17

My newborn daughter inspired my first book, *The Parable of the Princesses.* I wanted her to understand her divinity and divine potential. As I look at the world all of my children are growing up in, I want them to have more than just knowledge. I want them to be armed with the shield of faith and the sword of the Spirit that will protect that knowledge and keep it always before their eyes and burning in their hearts.

The fiery darts of the adversary—temptations—are being showered down upon us constantly. We are taught in the scriptures that the danger of these fiery darts is their ability to "overpower [us] unto blindness" (1 Nephi 15:24). When we start taking even little steps off the pathway, we leave our shield of faith behind, and we are sure to be hit by the adversary's fiery darts. They immediately weaken our vision, and we begin to forget where we were going.

It is easy to see that much of the world has become blinded and is living far beneath their eternal potential. Nephi prophesied of our day, saying, "At that day shall [the devil] rage in the hearts of the children of men, and stir them up to anger against that which is good. And others will he pacify, and lull them away into carnal security . . . and thus the devil cheateth their souls, and leadeth them away carefully down to hell" (2 Nephi 28:20–21).

Despite all the confusion and wickedness that rages in the world, the pathway to the Kingdom of Light is clear and strong and true for all who seek it. There is nothing more inspiring than seeing someone traveling that pathway with conviction and confidence, wearing the armor of God.

As we are taught in the scriptures, the sword of the Spirit represents the word of God. As we read and study the scriptures daily, the Spirit will strengthen us and increase our desire to stay on the pathway. We will be inspired by disciples of Christ who were true to the pathway. Our faith will be kindled, and it will be harder for us to forget the destination.

The invitation of this book is to come and travel with those going to the Kingdom of Light. The journey is real. Our loving Heavenly Father is real. We can travel with His mighty protection and power. He will help us if we seek Him. His way is the only way to life, to light, to love, and to joy.

To the Kingdom of Light!

Resources on JennyPhillips.com

Visit JennyPhillips.com for sheet music to the songs in this book, ideas for using this book with youth activities, Family Home Evening lesson plans, and more!

About the Author

Jenny Phillips is one of the most sought after and active performing artists in the Latter-day Saint music industry. She has released several albums and performed across the United States and internationally at more than a thousand performances in nineteen countries. Stories of change and testimony follow wherever she goes.

After graduating from Brigham Young University, Jenny released her first album independently. Today, as one of the top-selling artists under Deseret Book's music label, Shadow Mountain Records, Jenny has become known throughout the world for her inspiring presentations and music for the youth of the Church.

Jenny's music has been translated into fourteen different languages and has also been performed by LDS youth groups in more than twenty-four nations.

In addition to her five full-length albums, Jenny has released six best-selling albums for LDS youth. *The Parable of the Golden Pathway* is her second book.

Jenny lives in North Salt Lake with her husband and three children.

Visit Jenny at www.jennyphillips.com.

About the Illustrator

Dan Burr earned a bachelor's degree in fine arts at Utah State University and a master's degree in illustration from Syracuse University. He and his wife, Patti, live with their two children and numerous animals on twelve acres of riverbottom in Tetonia, Idaho, a setting that provides a lot of artistic inspiration. Dan Burr's illustrations and fine artwork can be viewed at www.danburr.com.